P9-CTA-822

snug

To Ellen, Hope, Judith, Lee, Lisa, Marni, and Julia
for the wisdom of your whimsy and the warmth of your hugs. —**M. E. H.**

For my snug Lachlan.
And for Miguel, Björn, Jared, Emmet, Jesse, and their Mamas. —**C. M. T.**

SIMON & SCHUSTER BOOKS FOR YOUNG READERS

An imprint of Simon & Schuster Children's Publishing Division
1230 Avenue of the Americas, New York, New York 10020

Text copyright © 1998 by Mary Elizabeth Hanson
Illustrations copyright © 1998 by Cheryl Munro Taylor
All rights reserved including the right of reproduction in whole or in part in any form.
SIMON & SCHUSTER BOOKS FOR YOUNG READERS is a trademark of Simon & Schuster.
Book design by Heather Wood. The text for this book is set in Stone Informal.
The illustrations were created with hand-cut, hand-colored, and handmade papers.
Printed and bound in Hong Kong by South China Printing Co. (1988) Ltd.
10 9 8 7 6 5 4 3 2 1 First Edition

Library of Congress Cataloging-in-Publication Data
Hanson, Mary Elizabeth.
Snug / by Mary Elizabeth Hanson ; illustrated by Cheryl Munro Taylor
p.   cm.
Summary: A mother bear patiently rescues her mischievous cub when he
gets into one difficulty after another while playing instead of learning to hunt.
ISBN 0-689-81164-0 [1. Bears-Fiction. 2. Behavior-Fiction.
3. Mother and child-Fiction.] I. Taylor, Cheryl Munro, date, ill. II. Title.
PZ7.H1988Sn 1998   [E]-dc21   96-44996   CIP   AC

mary elizabeth hanson

snug

illustrated by cheryl munro taylor

Simon & Schuster
Books for Young Readers

hidden by leaves, Snug
sneaks up on Mother.

She sniffs the ground
and the bear cub
pounces.

"Playtime!" he squeals.

"No," says Mother.
"Time for a lesson."

She takes Snug to a meadow where corn lilies grow, and shows him how to dig up the bulbs.

But Snug does not care. A frog hops past his snout.

Snug hops too. He bounds over flowers. He soars over trees and mountains like an eagle.

He is wild. He is powerful. He is...

under Mother's paw.

"Time to wrestle?"

"No, Snug," sighs Mother.
"Time for a snack."

"Yes!" says Snug. "A
snack!"

Mother leads him to a tree and finds an anthill. Snug watches as she scrapes away the soil and lays her paw upon it. She lets the ants run over her toes, then slurps them up.

"I'd rather eat beetles," mutters Snug, sniffing the tree's bark.

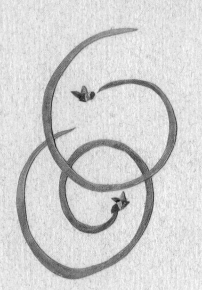

A chipmunk scurries down the trunk
and scampers away.

Snug scampers too.

With flashing fox feet, he chases the
scoundrel. The chipmunk darts into a
hollow log. Snug follows. The chipmunk
chirps and skitters out the other end.
Dusty darkness closes in on Snug, but
he presses forward.

He is bold. He is fearless. He is...

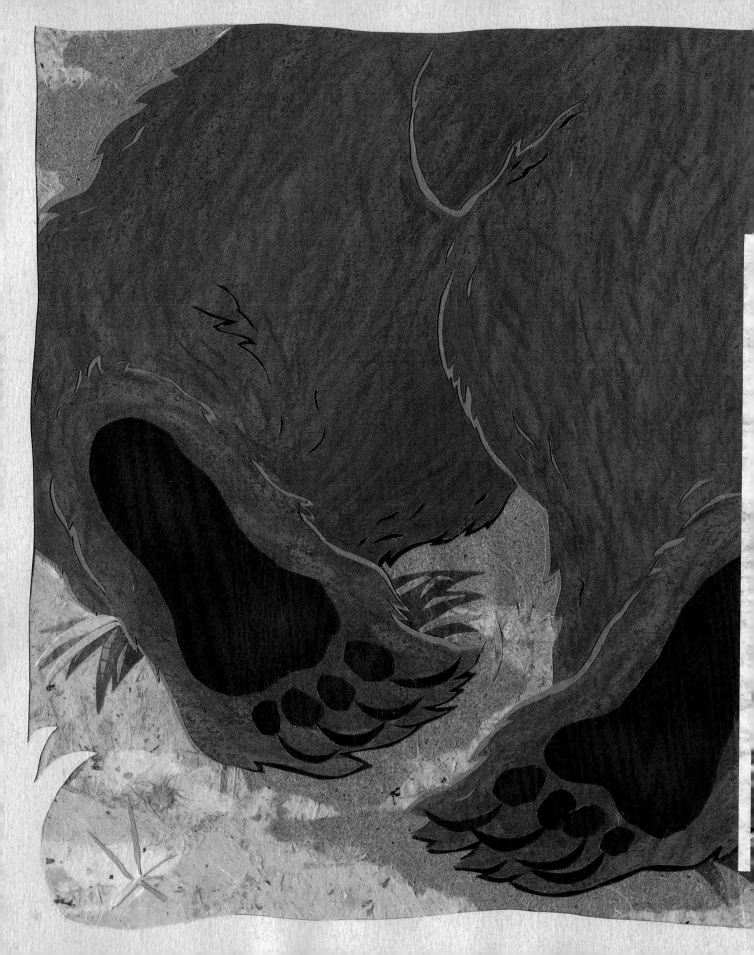

stuck.

He tries to escape, but the log gets tighter. He will have to live there. All alone. With nothing to eat.

"Muh! Muh! MUH!"

Snug is still crying when something grabs his tail. It hurts, and he yelps as he is pulled backward.

Once free, he nuzzles Mother. She grunts and lumbers through the woods toward the river's edge.

Snug follows.
"Now can we play?"

"No, Snug," she grumbles.
"You must learn to fish."

Snug trundles behind her.
Fishing might be fun.

But not like Mother does it. She just stands there, watching and swatting fish.

"Shouldn't we chase them?"

A silver trout darts between his stubby legs and swims away into the murmuring water.

Snug swims too. Swift as an otter, he splashes after the fish. The river pulls him toward a noisy waterfall but Snug is not frightened.

He is brave. He is daring. He is...

going too fast.

But Mother is faster and she snatches him up in her mouth. She swims to the shore and drops him on his bottom.

"You need a nap," she growls.

"I need to play!" cries Snug.

Mother snarls and chases him into a pine tree.
Snug curls up between two strong limbs and
Mother goes hunting.

Snug hunts too. High in the tree, he spies a sleeping blue jay.

He uncurls and climbs to the bird's perch. With the grace of a mountain lion, Snug slinks to the end of the branch. The blue jay wakes with a screech. Snug slips. He claws at the sky and grabs the branch.

He is quick.
He is clever.
He is...

upside down.

"Muh?"

But Mother is gone.

The angry blue jay screams and dives at Snug. Other jays gather to scold him. He tries to swat the birds, but they jab with sharp beaks. Snug peeks at the ground far below. Mother is back. She does not look happy, but she will not jab him. He lets go of the limb.

Wriggling and squealing, he tumbles through the air.

Then, ploomf! He lands on a pine needle pillow and rolls down the hill. He crashes into a stump, shakes his head, and looks up to find Mother rolling too. More frightening than a flood, she is coming for Snug.

She is mighty, she is fierce, she is...

wrestling and rumbling and playing with Snug.